The Moon Might Be Milk

LISA SHULMAN

illustrated by

WILL HILLENBRAND

DUTTON CHILDREN'S BOOKS

to Daniel,
BEST WISHES!
Will Hillenbrand
2010

For Mariah, who wondered
—L.S.

To Lisa, who has
the patience of an angel!
—W.H.

DUTTON CHILDREN'S BOOKS • A division of Penguin Young Readers Group
Published by the Penguin Group • Penguin Group (USA) Inc., 375 Hudson Street,
New York, New York 10014, U.S.A. • Penguin Group (Canada), 90 Eglinton Avenue East,
Suite 700, Toronto, Ontario, Canada M4P 2Y3 (a division of Pearson Penguin Canada
Inc.) • Penguin Books Ltd, 80 Strand, London WC2R 0RL, England • Penguin Ireland,
25 St Stephen's Green, Dublin 2, Ireland (a division of Penguin Books Ltd) • Penguin
Group (Australia), 250 Camberwell Road, Camberwell, Victoria 3124, Australia
(a division of Pearson Australia Group Pty Ltd) • Penguin Books India Pvt Ltd,
11 Community Centre, Panchsheel Park, New Delhi - 110 017, India • Penguin Group
(NZ), Cnr Airborne and Rosedale Roads, Albany, Auckland 1310, New Zealand
(a division of Pearson New Zealand Ltd) • Penguin Books (South Africa) (Pty) Ltd,
24 Sturdee Avenue, Rosebank, Johannesburg 2196, South Africa •
Penguin Books Ltd, Registered Offices: 80 Strand, London WC2R 0RL, England

Text copyright © 2007 by Lisa Shulman
Illustrations copyright © 2007 by Will Hillenbrand

Library of Congress Cataloging-in-Publication Data

Shulman, Lisa.
The moon might be milk / by Lisa Shulman ; illustrated by Will Hillenbrand.—1st ed.
   p. cm.
Summary: A young girl asks her animal friends what they think the moon is made of,
and her grandmother proves that each theory is partly correct. Includes recipe.
ISBN-13: 978-0-525-47647-4
ISBN-10: 0-525-47647-4 (hardcover)
[1. Moon—Fiction. 2. Cookies—Fiction. 3. Grandmothers—Fiction. 4. Animals—Fiction.]
I. Hillenbrand, Will, ill. II. Title.
PZ7.S559444Moo 2006
[E]—dc22   2005032750

Published in the United States by Dutton Children's Books,
a division of Penguin Young Readers Group
345 Hudson Street, New York, New York 10014
www.penguin.com/youngreaders

Designed by IRENE VANDERVOORT

Manufactured in China   First Edition

10 9 8 7 6 5 4 3 2 1

The night was almost gone, and a large round moon sank in the sky. Its bright light poured through the window, waking Rosie.

"Look at the moon," she said to Cat. "I wonder what it's made of."

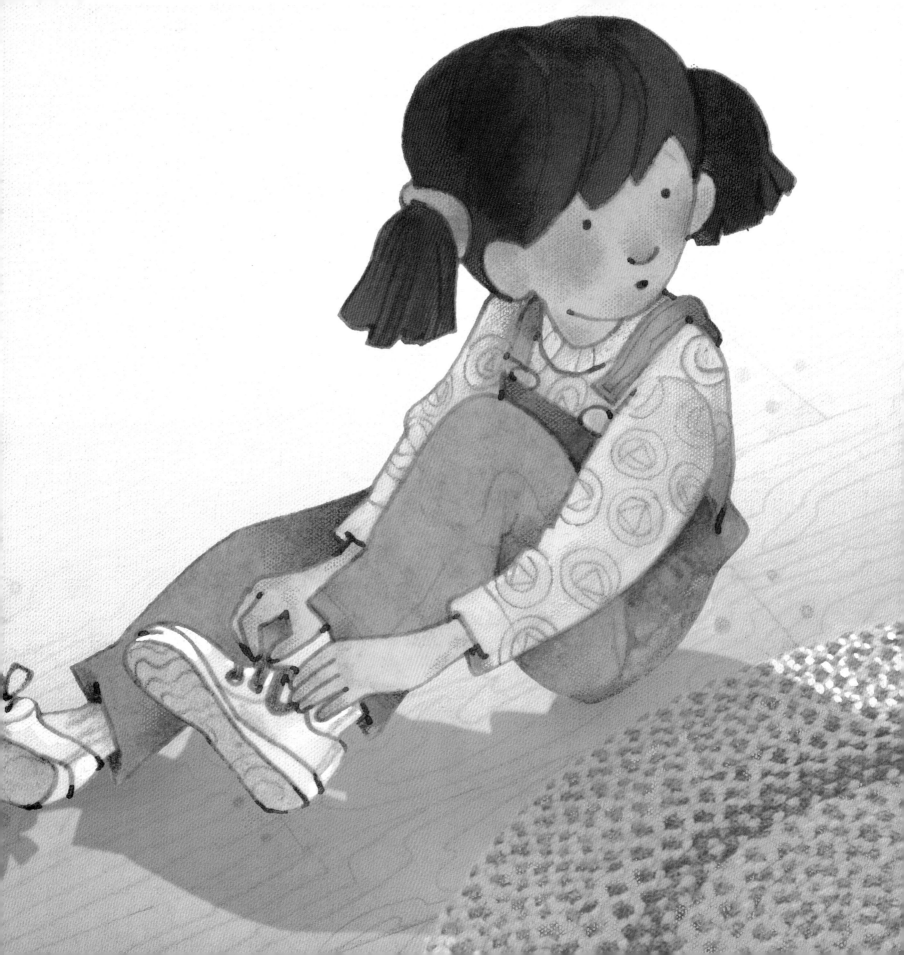

Cat stretched lazily. "The moon is a saucer of fresh milk," he purred. "It spills from the sky into puddles on the ground."

"The moon might be milk," Rosie said. "But it might not."

"Then let's ask Hen," said Cat.

When the sun had risen, Rosie and Cat set off. They walked and they walked until they came to Hen.

"Hello, Hen," said Rosie. "Can you tell us what the moon is made of? Cat thinks it's a saucer of milk."

"Milk?" cackled Hen. "Oh my dear, no. The moon is an egg. Small shining chicks hatch from it to become the stars."

"The moon might be an egg," Rosie said. "But it might not."

"Then let's ask Butterfly," said Hen.

So Rosie and Cat and Hen went on until they came to Butterfly. "Hello, Butterfly," said Rosie. "Can you tell us what the moon is made of? Cat thinks it's a saucer of milk, and Hen says it's an egg."

"Oh no," whispered Butterfly. "The moon is made of sugar. It's sticky and sparkling and oh, so sweet."

"The moon might be sugar," Rosie said. "But it might not."

"Then let's ask Dog," said Butterfly.

So Rosie and Cat and Hen and Butterfly went on until they came to Dog.

"Hello, Dog," said Rosie. "Can you tell us what the moon is made of? Cat thinks it's a saucer of milk, Hen says it's an egg, and Butterfly believes it's made of sugar."

"The moon," said Dog with a wag of his tail, "is a round pat of sweet, creamy butter." And he licked his lips with his long pink tongue.

"The moon might be butter," Rosie said. "But it might not."

"Then let's ask Mouse," said Dog.

So Rosie and Cat and Hen and Butterfly and Dog went on. Soon they came upon Mouse scurrying back to her hole.

"Hello, Mouse," said Rosie. "Can you tell us what the moon is made of? Cat thinks it's a saucer of milk, Hen says it's an egg, Butterfly believes it's made of sugar, and Dog tells us it's a pat of butter."

"You're all wrong," grumbled Mouse, anxious to be on her way. "The moon is made of white flour. When the wind blows, it makes great powdery clouds in the sky."

"The moon might be flour," Rosie said. "But it might not."

"Well then, what do *you* think it is?" asked Mouse impatiently.

Rosie thought for a moment. "I'm not sure," she said at last. "But maybe Gran will know." She ran off toward her grandmother's house, with Cat and Hen and Butterfly and Dog and even grumbling Mouse close behind.

"Gran?" Rosie pushed open the kitchen door.

"Your grandmother's not here, but a bit of the moon is," said Dog.

"See how the moon shines," said Butterfly.

"How white it is," purred Cat.

"And so smooth." Hen clucked approvingly.

Mouse nibbled a hole in the flour sack. "Ah, moon clouds! Just like I told you," she said proudly.

Just then, Rosie's grandmother came in. "Rosie!" she said. "What a surprise! And what's all this?"

"I guess it's the moon," Rosie answered.

"The moon?"

"Gran," said Rosie, "I've been looking all day for someone who can tell me what the moon is made of."

"What have you learned?" Gran set a bowl on the table.

"Mouse thinks the moon is made of flour."

"It *is* flour," Mouse said importantly.

"Perhaps it is," said Gran, measuring flour into the bowl.

"And Dog tells me the moon is a pat of butter," Rosie continued.

"That's right!" said Dog.

"It's possible," Gran said as she put butter into another bowl.

"But Butterfly believes the moon is made of sugar," said Rosie.

"Well, she could be right," Gran said as she mixed sugar with the butter.

"And Hen says the moon's an egg, and Cat thinks it's milk."

"It might be an egg," said Gran, cracking an egg into the butter and sugar. "But then again, it might be milk." She added milk to the bowl, then stirred in the flour.

Rosie watched with excitement as Gran dropped rounded spoonfuls of the dough onto a baking sheet, flattened them, and sprinkled them with sugar.

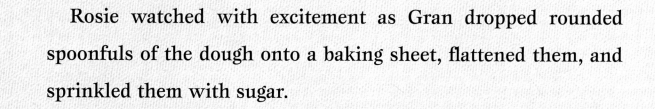

As her grandmother slid the tray into the oven, Rosie burst out,
"Gran! I know what you're making!"

Gran smiled as the kitchen began to fill with the sweet scent
of baking.

"Flour, butter, sugar, egg, and milk," Rosie said, ticking off the
ingredients on her fingers. "Gran, you've made the moon!"

"The moon!" cried the animals. Gran opened the oven door and pulled out a tray of sparkling moon-shaped cookies. Gran passed them around while Rosie poured tea.

"So the moon is made of milk!" purred Cat.

"And egg," cackled Hen.

"And sugar," whispered Butterfly.

"And butter," said Dog.

"Well, I was right, too," said Mouse, nibbling at her cookie. "The moon is made of flour."

"Rosie, what do you think?" asked Gran.

Rosie took a bite of her warm cookie and brushed the crumbs from her mouth. "I think the moon is a great big sugar cookie in the night sky," she said at last.

The animals nodded in agreement. Rosie took another bite and looked out the window. The sun's rays were spreading over the hills like melting butter.

"Look at the sun," Rosie said. "I wonder what *it's* made of."

Gran's Sugar Cookie Moons

2 cups all-purpose flour
1 1/2 teaspoons baking powder
1/2 teaspoon salt
1/2 cup soft butter
1 cup sugar
1 egg
2 tablespoons milk
1 teaspoon vanilla

1. Preheat oven to 375 degrees. Grease a cookie sheet.

2. Stir together flour, baking powder, and salt.

3. In another bowl, mix butter and sugar. Stir in egg, milk, and vanilla.

4. Add dry ingredients to butter mixture and mix well.

5. Drop dough by rounded teaspoonfuls 2 inches apart on greased cookie sheet.

6. To flatten each cookie and make it sparkle, grease the bottom of a glass. Dip the glass into sugar and press it onto the dough.

7. Bake 10 to 12 minutes.